LITTLE BIRDS

Copyright © 2023 by the individual authors
Designed by Ira Rat

This is a work of fiction. Names, characters, businesses, places, events, locales, and incidents are either the products of the author's imagination or used in a fictitious manner. Any resemblance to actual persons, living or dead, or actual events is purely coincidental.

This book may not be reproduced in whole or in part, except for the inclusion of brief quotations in a review, without permission in writing from the author or publisher. No part of this publication may be reproduced, stored in or introduced into retrieval system, or transmitted, in any form, or by any means (electronic, mechanical, photocopying, recording, or otherwise), without prior permission of the publisher.

Requests for permission should be directed to
filthylootpress@gmail.com

LITTLE BIRDS

SHY WATSON 05 • **GARTH MIRÓ** 10 • **CHARLENE ELSBY** 16 • **JACK SKELLEY** 27 • **DANIELLE CHELOSKY** 47

filthyloot.com

2AM IN BROWNSVILLE

Shy Watson

The first time Jordan and I had sex, he grabbed a magnum condom from the 50-count box on the ground beside us, slid it over his vaguely hard average-sized penis, and played the pilot episode of The Sopranos. Jordan was a mattress-on-the-floor guy, and he had stopped paying rent a few months back, but he had promised me lentils and toast if I "braved" the brisk 10-minute walk to his apartment. We had only met once, at the park between our neighborhoods, but I had mentioned being hungry over text.

Jordan lit a post-coital cigarette and contemplatively stared at the ceiling.

"My ex was a Nazi," he said.

"What?"

"We were engaged." I let the weight of the statement wash over me, though he was only 22—five years my junior—and it was hard to take the prospect of him as a fiancé seriously. "She got on all these blogs," he continued, "real evil shit, then started inviting neckbeards to our house down in Ditmas Park."

"Oh cool," I said, "You lived in Ditmas."

"Yeah, we were engaged. You actually follow her on Instagram."

"Who?"

"I'd rather not say."

I was unaware that I followed a Nazi on Instagram. Perhaps I didn't. Perhaps Jordan didn't know the difference between an edgelord and a Nazi. Perhaps I didn't. Maybe there was no difference. Either way, I didn't care about his former fiancée, and it occurred to me that this unsolicited confession could be some misguided attempt to make me jealous. Jordan ashed his cigarette onto the crotch flap of the boxers he was wearing. He suddenly seemed capable of anything.

"So have you talked to your landlord yet?" I asked, desperate to change the subject.

"No, but I'm banking on the eviction moratorium. I can't be expected to barista when Little Skips is shut down."

"Why don't you apply for unemployment?"

"Because I'm not a fucking bottom feeder."

In that moment, I decided I would never return to Jordan's apartment. In fact, I would not even sleep there, but would instead "brave" the brisk walk home, even if it was 2am in Brownsville.

Jordan leaned over and cracked the window, for which I was grateful. The Sopranos droned on in the background. It was the part where Dr. Melfi analyzed Tony's love of the ducks, the part where she inferred he wanted to protect his family.

"That was distracting," I said.

"What was?"

"The Sopranos. I've never watched it, so it was distracting. That's why I didn't come." The Sopranos had nothing to do with why I didn't come, but I felt I owed him an explanation, as he had overextended himself while vigorously fingering me with the candor of a preteen.

"Oh," he said, "I've seen it so many times it's like elevator music to me."

I imagined myself on an elevator with gray carpeted walls, a square shaped mirror above my head. I gazed up at my reflection as gun shots and car chases blasted through the speakers. Each passing floor was just another floor down, and there was no hope of getting off.

I sprung from the mattress and excused myself. Every time I had sex with a new partner, I instantly contracted a UTI. The trick was to pee afterwards. Jordan's toilet seat was lifted and shit stained the bowl. A neglected litter box rested under the sink, though I had not witnessed any other evidence of a cat. I lowered the lid and dressed it in toilet paper before planting my ass.

My urethra burned as I forced a jerky stream that stopped and started like an engine turning over in the dead of winter. As I relieved myself, I navigated to Jordan's Instagram and surveyed our mutuals. There were only five women we both followed, and none of them seemed the least bit like Nazis. I wiped from front to back then gazed at my blonde hair and blue eyes in Jordan's toothpaste-studded mirror. Maybe he was the real Nazi. Maybe he just wanted to see what I'd say.

When I returned to Jordan's room, he had just lit another cigarette. I got on my knees in search of my crumpled panties, found them, then dressed.

"Where do you think you're going?" Jordan said.

"Home." I squeezed the side button on my iPhone to light the screen. "It's getting late and I have to work in the morning."

Jordan took a long drag from his cigarette and said "Suit yourself," then gave me an unsettling salute as I turned to leave his room.

HOW TO LOSE AND WIN

Garth Miró

My luck has been alarmingly good lately. I'm not the one who's supposed to write this. She dropped out. It's now one forty-five in the morning, and all I can think is: how much can I really make writing about Joan Didion's auction? How far is God going to go with this? The luck. Hopefully, just enough to cover my bids and no more—I still have a massive golem of a habit.

I click on one of the items. Lot 123. A group of Didion's notebooks, blank. Maybe with the right one of these totems, surely imbued with her cool contemptuous laughter towards Fate, my luck will get fed up and jump tracks. I'll stop getting these jobs that keep me a comfortable junky.

12 days left in the auction.

The next morning, I'm excited to bid a hundred dollars for Lot 111, a set of four old Philip Guston catalogs. I have a feeling they must be soaked in the exact type of luck-castrating aura I'm looking for. I'm immediately outbid by twenty dollars. Somehow, I know it's a man I'm up against; something about the bid, the tackiness of the desperation. I can use that. Channel Didion. She knew how to seduce. She was certainly unsentimental, but I don't think she'd be particularly happy seeing a tacky desperate man like this walking away with her stuff. So, it's my duty. I'd simply kill him if I could. If we could just get over our squeamishness, that sort of approach would solve most problems around money.

Bid, then outbid. This freak must really be terrified. The poor rich bastard; nothing's more detrimental than a life of pure wins. I need to divert my energies, find a new item not so contested. I start to form an idea. I begin tracking his bids across new Lots, locating him each time by identifying his incessant pattern of twenty-dollar raises. I will make him suffer.

11 days.

The afternoon is uncharacteristically hot for

November. The living river of rats starts to flow again, optimistically scurrying from one rotting pile to the next. (My idea grows bigger.) I don't think Didion was much used to rats, growing up wealthy in Sacramento. She was rich, sure. But not like my nemesis. She was also born into a time when rich women were expected to stay inside, slowly buried under the fabulous gifts their husbands brought home to smooth over fucking the new typist on floor three. Didion used her wealth to her advantage. Entering rooms filled with breeds of human us American peasants will never see, but feel the consequences of, writing them and all their deformities into the spotlight. She confirmed what we all knew—that it was rats in those rooms. Her critics now probably look at these bidding items, coveted by Account Managers, trinkets that Media Execs will place on their mantels and point to during bland dinner parties, and smile smugly. See? This auction is wealth and status and nothing more came out of it. I'm sure her critics are satisfied this is where it all ended up. Dilettantes collecting junk. But at least Didion's stuff draws out the Managerial class, so that they may be identified. Yes, if my plan goes right, of crossing all lines, I can at least ruin one of them.

10 more days.

I go into Lot 126, a late Victorian carved mahogany side chair, and raise my nemesis by twenty-five dollars. I imagine Didion sitting there at her writing desk (Lot 23, three thousand dollars), hungover. I am hungover. Here he comes, twenty more dollars. I bid right back, another twenty-five on top of that. I drive my nemesis into a frenzy. I force him to pour every ounce of attention into beating me.

The next morning, I find my man at each of his now-obsessed-over Lots. I'll keep raising until the very last moment—and then let him win. It's only right. To let a winner keep doing what he was born into.

Day 5, he's surely starting to miss work. My relentless bids are locking him at the computer every minute of every day in a frustrated rage. My twenty-fives pounding him one after another, big meaty bids in his face.

Bid. Raise. I'm always there. He's already insane. He hates me more than I hate him. He'll lose his job by Wednesday. We're glued to our screens. I'm possessed by the ghost of Didion, both of us laughing at this man's new world. "I'm fucking leaving," his trophy wife will say by day 6. He'll try and hide it. But by Thursday next week, she'll be taking the kids. For the support check. He won't send them a dime—that would eat into his bidding funds. To combat me. A winner can't lose, no matter what he has to lose to win. Maybe, if I'm really lucky he'll go to jail. On Friday, after one last plea to come to his senses, the wife will hurry the kids out the door with suitcases, him still frantically clicking, red, sweating globules, locked at the computer. He won't notice them leave.

5 days.

It's four-thirty in the afternoon. We're neck and neck on a late federal walnut table. I've been following the money.

2 days.

It's her Celine glasses taking the cake. Everyone's made a concerted effort to raise the price. Twenty-thousand dollars. Sunglasses. I raise. Twenty-thousand and twenty-five.

1 day.

I imagine Didion taking the flatware, now going for seven grand, and cutting the faces off all the men in her way, who control all the words in all the books.

I make one more bid. All together, with everything added up, we're in at something like 900,025. My nemesis is clicking and clicking and clicking. When the auction closes, I can almost hear him screaming, somewhere, in the dark of a room, alone, the computer glowing against his bloodshot eyes.

I lose. No, I win.

THE LILLIANS

Charlene Elsby

When I was eight or nine years old, I remember my parents taking me to my uncle's house to meet his new girlfriend. They smoked cigarettes at the kitchen table and drank beer from the can while she drank wine from a wine glass, and even though her lipstick stayed red all night and her hair was sprayed in place and she laughed at all their jokes, even so despite all that my dad turned to my mom on the way home in the car and said, "She looks like she's never had an orgasm in her life."

I didn't know what he meant by that, but looking across the table now, I definitely do. My colleagues decided we'd go out, get to know each other on a personal level. I pictured drinks and dancing. We were meeting at a bar, and here I'd put my hair up and got my tits out while across the table, this woman just sat there in her work clothes with her fucking son and sat there, having conceived him without ever having orgasmed, and I looked at his face to see if you could tell from it the joyless sex from which he was spawned, and there it was, written all over it. Intergenerational prudishness.

I drank my vodka and Diet Coke for a nice, clean drunk that wouldn't stop me working in the morning. Lillian said she had to go home early anyway, so she didn't think she'd have to find a sitter for little Dylan. After all, no one would mind. It's just so hard to make time for everything what with performing the duties expected of her based on her gender role and also holding down a full-time job like she's some fucking feminist hero for ruining vodka night.

Lillian was explaining how the same principle applied when she'd left work early that day, like she did every day, explaining that she had to pick up her kid like there weren't any way around it, like there weren't people who had always worked and had always had kids and had never thought to think that it didn't make them special. Having it all is for people with the money for it. Anyway, Lillian picked up her kid and took him to the salon, and now he's sitting there with a fucking $200 haircut looking like he'd never grow up to fuck anyone or if he did, he'd do it from behind as he buried their face in a pillow so they wouldn't hear him say, "Mommy" as he came. Meanwhile, Lillian explained how it was so much easier for her, not having to find childcare, just bringing him to the salon with her, letting them work on him at the same time as she got her own hair done, and because that made it so much easier for her to find the time.

"Of course," I told her. "It's totally worth it when you factor in how much your time is worth," I said.

As if no one else had mastered the art of finding the time, which really means, to people like Lillian, that they took the time. They fucking took it, and they took it from the rest of us. The ones who had to cover for her after she left shift to go take her wiener son to the salon. But people like Lillian grew up in a framework where such phrases were comprehensible, where people found the time and told themselves they didn't take it, that they'd found it, where such egregious indecencies were so well covered up within her milieu that she not only believed what she was saying, she assumed we all did too.

There were a lot of her, here in the lower middle

class.

Ever since I'd been promoted well beyond my birthright, there they were. The Lillians. They spoke a different dialect and spent a different sort of money, different from what I made. Not because our salaries were different, but because they didn't need theirs. She took the time from the rest of us, because she needed it to grease her son's head enough to crawl back inside her pussy after ten years on the outside. You know he's never been comfortable out here. He's always been a sensitive boy.

"Tell them about my game," it said.

"I have to tell you about Dylan's game," Lillian said, and told us all about how not only did Dylan play a game of baseball, he actually swung the bat this time when the ball headed in his direction and, even though he didn't hit it, he was still her little wiener.

Sorry.

Little winner.

And the fact that Dylan thought that when she shared that story, we'd all be impressed, told me something about his home life too. The kind where every good was rewarded and every misstep swept under the rug. The rug was probably purchased with two months' worth of my salary, but Lillian decided that it was worth it, because of how it brought the house together, and we didn't want Dylan growing up in a broken home, now did we.

You see, Lillian was a feminist, but her husband didn't like that, and off he went. She was a feminist, because she had a job she didn't need. She fought for the right to work, like it was a privilege, like it wasn't something thrust upon us as a way to make the rent. Do your suffering, take the money, do it again until such time as the value of your labour decreases sufficiently relative to your compensation that the company decides it is in both of your best interests to retire and die as quickly as possible thereafter.

After all, the pension fund was dwindling.

But Lillian didn't need the work; she would have been just fine. And because she had the option not to, she thought it was more noble of her to do the work, to do most of the work, when she had the time, when she was there, when she didn't have a salon appointment for both her and her son at the same time, so that she wouldn't have to go through the suffering of having to find someone to care for her child without giving him a fucking two hundred dollar wash cut style but, after all, it was worth it and you deserve it because oh my dear you've been through so much it has been a rough year oh my goodness your strength is so inspiring.

Fuck you, ya have, Lillian.

Fuck off, so I can get another vodka without anyone mentioning how late it was getting and how we all had to be up in the morning and how it was our responsibility to take care of ourselves because we self-sufficient ladies had to take care of ourselves. In my mind, I made a wanking motion in her direction, like we used to do when someone was a worthless jackoff.

I thought of the work I could be doing and whether I wouldn't be better off, back at the restaurants and the factories, destroying my joints but at least staying thin from the labour and the cigarettes, the uppers when we had them. I used to look at the office ladies with their air conditioning and wonder if I wouldn't be better off as one of them, and now as Lillian is crying and we all have to tell her it's all right, she's so strong, she'll make it through the night again, I wonder if I've made a huge mistake.

I waved the waiter down and bought shots for the table, but by the horrified looks on their faces when the tiny glasses arrived, I had to conclude that office ladies do other things than shots to make themselves feel better. So while Stacey tried to convince Lillian that her looks were not yet gone, and while Alison convinced her that a short cut was just as beautiful as her long hair used to be and that besides, a real man would still love her with short hair and some fucking pussy boy child besides, I took four shots of whiskey with a Diet Coke and vodka chaser.

Lillian would have made the server take them back.

No matter that they couldn't pour it back into the bottle or sell it to anyone else, she'd make them take it back, because you're allowed to return the things you purchase and that's just how it is, she thought.

But that isn't how it is, is it?

I looked around for servers to empathize with, to look at in that way that let them know that I shouldn't be here, that I was one of them, and that

I didn't know these women, not really. Not how they worked or didn't, not what their guiding motivations were, and certainly not why they'd brought some kid slathered in pomade into a bar on a fucking Tuesday.

Some water showed up at the table and while I didn't appreciate the sentiment, I did enjoy putting moisture back in my mouth.

And then I looked at Dylan.

He couldn't be having fun, either, his Mom taking him out first to the salon and then to the bar after school. I tried to imagine him suffering, sitting on the rug which I imagined as the focal point of their suburban home in the subdivision built five years ago on the edge of town, too expensive for the wages of most of us except that if you lived there you could drive for forty minutes to a city where much better people worked. I pictured Dylan coming home from school, sitting on the rug, turning on his video game, my consciousness inserting into the image an old Nintendo system, like the one we used to have but just because somebody found a sale or a deal or an employee discount or grandma bought it. I saw Dylan getting distracted by despair and putting the controller down to cry, wondering where his father had gone and what feminism was and whether it was worth it.

I saw the real Dylan pull out his phone and start playing with it, the sound grating against the voices at the table, the other voices in the room, the music on the stereo and the television above the bar. Over all that sound, my chair against the floor still caught the attention of my colleagues as I pushed it back and slowly nudged it closer and closer to Dylan where we'd been abandoned at the kids' end of the table.

"What are you playing?" I asked him.

"Youtube," is what he said.

"Do you want to go home, Dylan?" I asked him. "Because I can make that happen."

Dylan nodded and said, "Yeah."

I nodded too and sealed the deal.

Now I wasn't left-handed, but that's where Dylan was, and I was stealthy.

"Watch this," I said and took a set of cutlery off the table, one which some poor server had wrapped up in a napkin at the end of their last shift, a napkin that they'd folded neatly around the standard set of knife fork spoon, and which they sealed with a little strip of paper that was sticky at one end. I took the knife and spoon, and I set them on the table on my left and right. I looked at all my colleagues still embedded in the script, some series of words and phrases that they'd learned from I don't know where but which were oft repeated and by now become habitual. The script which we all had to learn while they just knew it, knew it from birth, because it came with the money and the good upbringing that entailed. They were boring.

The middle class is fucking boring, is what I thought as I took the fork in my left hand and jammed it into Dylan's thigh.

Of course, he started crying, and then it was time to go.

Lillian explained that he'd always been a sensitive boy and that anyway, he'd been through a lot. The image of him crying in that haircut made me laugh although I shouldn't but they'd never ever think to know that that's what was so funny.

I walked outside after an extended period of putting coats on, during which Dylan had stopped crying and gone back to turning up the volume on his phone. As my colleagues got in their cars, I said I'd take an uber, and I waved as I told them, drive away, that I'll be fine. Then I went right back inside and ordered vodka. I took it to the bathroom, having had to pee for now over an hour, and I set my drink on the toilet paper holder, like a lady. On the door, I used an office pen to scratch a message on top of all the other messages left behind by women like me.

Fuck the Lillians, is what I wrote.

Fuck them all to hell and see if that'll get them off.

WALT DISNEY'S HEAD

Jack Skelley

INTRODUCTION:

Whether I turn out to be the hero of my own life or just another dumb uncomprehending id this paper must prove. I mark its arc as clouds part and moons pop into Hollywood signs, where a dreamy creamy pearl arrows a clerestory window to spotlight a pile of books.

There, inscribed on her scholarship docs, were …

    1. Catalytic authorships

    2. Incantatory French theory

    3. Fake IDs

4. Fractal pronouns

5. Oracle alibis

6. Split infinities and wet-dream prophecies… all emanating from… the incident!

Yes, she defrosts the cryonic head of Walt Disney. She grasps the Transcendental Object at the End of Time – a mirror ball of myriad eyes glancing shards of evolution's end-point into the past – our present. And these saucers that spin the skies mandala a hole in my wholeness. My C.G. Jung youths alchemize a cradle for the human race, rocked by a caring presence. A loving hand of non-accidental evolution reaches Omega universality, where, in mêlées of his-and-her crania, our maternal golden age of hominids freely copulate to decapitate a grumpy usurper ego Yahweh.

And so, what straining for eternal life jibed with mass markets?

What frozen fire in the madhouse at the end of time confused us with the stars?

What post-mortem evolutions of brand, platonic yet carnal, ever sang in such precision?

What TikTok matrices of clout molested

umpteen to the 10th minds of Zoomers?

What gnosis of make-believe narcolized more worlds?

And what zombie free-enterprise feasted until zero hosts remained?

For when our cryo-inseminated brains unthawed, a million *dummkopfs* melted!

I hear her voice. She channels hallucino-botanist Terence McKenna: "Forever we approach an Eschaton already present. Easter morning compresses and concresses complexity to raise the curtain on computoid human consciousness."

And yet she struggles to complete her thesis, entitled *An Anatomy of Plastic Love*, telling me, alarmingly, "I sit down to write about love and no words come out because love makes me lose my head, and my head is where the words are."

ABSTRACT:

VASTLY!

A Gregor Samsara, I baptize in ice: Not, however, snug in the guts of California Institute of the Arts. That the brain would encase in this obvious place is "just a myth." Rather, awareness unfreezes in the 1966 Blue Bayou restaurant and Disneyland Club 33, a number fraught with Freemasonry. Aye! This zone floats duotone Arthur Rimbaud sneezing one-in-a-million vessels off-course, wacked and woozy: In the front seat rides a 10-year-old suburban Kundun gifted with great imagination, princess gowned in Aurora gold.

Still, in the steam-swirl of reverse cataracts, like a catastrophe dream groping below ground again and again, dodging tsunamis of fate, my "she-brain" outmaneuvered the heel-nipping of competitors and bureaucrats. More vicious were the fables – gruesome, vengeful, out for blood. These whirl and Kraken. I see them now: Pinocchium and Pocahontati with knives and ARs, snarling, oversexed and underdressed, as if in a lurid Robert Williams canvas. And yet her Disney head – solo, condensed in Alfred Whitehead's concrescence of all parts of self grown together – shot the curl under the docks of these grabby legends to surf southward, inward, pastward.

METHODOLOGY:
The Dead Sea Files

For eschatological migraine brain pain drain, the scalp is sliced, folded back, hair and all. The tiny circular saw whirrs. The cranium is windowed and set aside. The oatmeal cerebellum poked and prodded. The growth extracted.

But wait! It turns out the tumor is another brain! Tiny. Pulsing. Algorithmic. The real parasite hides inside <u>that</u> inner ego. Following this Manchurian implant swap, all materials are re-stitched. The hair regrows quickly. Best of all, this cranial procedure tightens her skin. Free facelift!

Malignant or benign, that's how Walt operates on the attention economy.

Therefore, take a break from mental fight. Get comfortable. Shut your eyes. Now, center sensation on the INSIDE of your lids. Slam into a black-light room zoom parading mazes, street grids, campuses, clusters of coruscant skyscrapers. Eidetic veins mutate, sizzle/squirm and day-glo into wallpaper shapes, from asphalt composite to every...

- Art Nouveau curl
- Deco edge
- Egyptian glyph
- Tiki grimace

- Quran-Muhaqqaq-script-cum-wildstyle-MTA-car-tag
- and Corningware cornflower-blue Mandarin dragon (both authentic and Orientalized)

…throughout art history and especially outside of it.

- Not to mention paisley nor tropical fish.

She sees these signs are birthed by more than intertextual graphic relationships. For everyone's eyelids vagina infinite (because infinitely morphing) dark-ride dioramas or Lewis Carroll Alice Coltrane dreamworld superstructures inside a mass-mind-mirror-maze.

The same with skin. There is feeling on the INSIDE of your skin. Feel that. Agro-rhythms attack neurons but cannot penetrate what's defended by letting go and simply feeling who YOU are, not what they tell you to be. The "THEY" forever attack until forever ends in now. Your synapses are heretical. They sizzle the revolution of electricity. Your YOU can replay their microscopic waves, because, after all, THEY are YOU. Everything is YOU. Reclaim it. It's yours anyway. Goddam hyper-entrepreneurs think they got us all, but we're always all US anyway. I mean

THEY I mean YOU. I mean I.

This is Arjuna's colorfield of battle with ugly SCOTUS faces or hideous Prezidunce heads… cartoon monsters that mask the face-rape of capital in ALL CAPS.

Zardozing above a California of racial memory, she of residual granite recalls this slasher-movie trope, biblical rebuke, and Bob Dylan lyric: Don't Look Back! You'll freeze into rock.

Thus my talismanic flight must free-range Madame Leota: Our Haunted Mansion medium (plus her bust besties crooning in the boneyard) hangs bodiless in mist to direct doom-buggy traffic and orchestras.

We alter the cranial climate in my rhetorical Walter.

In sacrifices to nothing by no one, in the darkest 64-Chan dungeons on the internet, where lurks the film of LBJ scalp-fucking JFK, is the magic kingdom of death.

And then they threw her down. Saint Cephalapor, Nike of Samothrace or Jezebel. And her blood splattered the walls and horses, and they trampled her, finding no more than her skull and feet and the palms of her hands.

Now she sings to the Amazonia Shuar tribe and their *tsantsas* – shrunken heads harvested as uncouth curios for Euro traders. The one Shuar leader who swapped heads for rifles promptly ambushed another war party, collecting more heads, buying more guns.

Tribe-tripping now, as acid skyrockets ferry over Bayou gators, Philippine Ifugao traders carry Jaguar Juice to Francis Coppola's Jungle Cruise of darkness. Damn the horror! I'm blinded by Marlon Brando pate! Through unsound methods, buried to the neck, merry Marie Antoinette is camo Martin Sheen, a voided face, rising from the Mekong Styx, steeped in stinky Southern Goth: "Ooooh, that smell! The smell of death surrounds you," sang Lynyrd Skynyrd in Falknerian rock.

I fly. I fly. I zoom your window by.

Say, did you catch mad Kanye's Isising of phantom Pete Davidson? The sword – like those birthed in Nam huts – rains justice upon the post-imperial decadence of twin towers, knifed precisely at their crowns, where the logos go.

Uneasy flies the head that capitalizes the dead.

For we see, dimension-wise, a Walt may

navigate subsidiaries, as Oliver Cromwell's head mercantiles time. Profiting through the imperial centuries, passing his dead head hand-to-hand, radical Restorationists with huge clipboards on their shoulders severed, spiked and effigied him in Westminster Hall. Blown by fog, sold and re-sold, tattered, toothless – a horrid antique, the head rose in price in the circuses and alleys of London.

Does a decaying gaze wield power over those who dare return the stare?

And if it's "just" a relic, why do relics stay when viewers pass away?

CONTEXTS:

Since I'm dead I give good head.

Whip some skull on me, Bitch Boi: My bronze noggin gong, my uvula bell, my skin port to Gnostic Empress **Barbelo** Barbarella and her sacramental "redemption by sin." For within her heresies the scatological becomes eschatological.

They guillotined "I love you." But they could not cut-off passion. Prone in place, mouthing baby sounds, they lock ASMRs in coo-pillow kisses.

Now anointing the Neverland sips of her nether holes are the lisping lips of **Khloe Kylie Kenner** and **Kim**. They huff and they fluff, with her plumping glosses for pre-verbal labial sacraments of glug-glug, gargle & gulp.

(By the way, by "me" I mean she. By "they" I mean we. And by "I" I mean you.)

Holy fuck! I'm a **super-hawt** augmented Agnes **Moorehead** with ass implants! I'm weird Bewitched bish Endora whose bolt-ons rebound double cc's of bubble trouble.

And I **eyerollgasm** a cosmology of cosmetology.

In the upper Juliet balcony I bow, butt up, and command:

- Lift this filly's flirty Tartan skirt.
- Scoop & swat my Walt twat!
- Careful, Romeo! You'll waterfall the floor with squish-squirt.

Hark! What yonder luscious lake windows holy heavens as we tally cums per encounter – maxing out one raunchy rally for a combined **13 !!!!!!!!** Throat-pie counts triple for degree of difficulty: slosh wash, snug rub, tug-bath shiatsu in the upper esophageal sphincter.

Their epiglottis was Medusalicious.

Her carnal superpowers.

Her boulder-hard Gorgon gaze.

Her endoscopic plunger.

Her magical freezing of spunk-rock retraction.

They may snake-charm a totem-pole for eons, poised and posed to re-re-RE-release Mommy's Daddy juice.

But just one look, and Medusa Mama stoned him out of his brain. Post-orgasmic blackout bliss lobotomized *La petite mort* unto *liebestod* – a kind of craniotomy removing the tumor of consciousness.

As they stare at the mirror, they indulge dualities of objectification. Not just brain to body, but face to self. And the self in all things.

Neurologically, biologically, is my face – the seat of my self – more spunkable than my physique? Might a skuzz-sloppy slut visage – eyes deadened in pleasure, tongue drivel dropping –

reflexively out-hawtify even the shapeliest torso snagged in fishnet of green neon?

THE FOREVER NOW OF AHEGAO

(pron: ah-heh-gah-oh)

In dummy face a love supreme

Of cross-eyed stupefied submission

Into exaltation, a gaze into a glaze,

Mindfulness into mindlessness,

A terrible sublimity is born,

And our barbarous Queen Barbelo

Beheads the hydra algorithm of capital.

Ooh la la! A super succulent *coup d'etat*.

For the difference is between how a severed head perceives – a subject – and how it appears – an object: **drawn as a figure**.

Etched in the disappearing ink of cunt nectar, the eloquence of **Hélène Cixous'** *ecriture feminine* became the numb-faced mouth prowess of **Sasha Grey**.

Her male counterpart, Garrett Brooks, AKA **Girth Brooks,** engorged, engulfed his face & cranium – lips, cheeks, hair. The image of head alone liberates. It annihilates the constraint of object-model. It takes flight.

And levitating betwixt, transcendent and bi-gendered, **Kimber James** stages hermaphrodesiac transformations toward Bimbo dominions.

The only way he gets off anally is from full-on face.

She mouthed her taint in mother tongue.

She knotted her hair and woman-handled her.

They coaxed love blood repeatedly.

And in a dead head's anguish of desire, babbling the glossolalia that precedes language, spirit re-palpitated.

In *The Greater Questions of Mary* (third century CE) Saint Epiphanius – bishop of Salamis and a compendium of suppressed texts – recounts this ritual of **godhead**:

> Mary took Jesus onto the mountain and prayed. He produced a woman from his side

and the three began to gratify. And when Jesus, dumbstruck and cum-struck, fell to the ground, Mary raised her up and said, "We believe earthly things, that we may know heavenly things. The emission comes to partake of that from which it came."

Till the age of thermonuclear **warheads** exacerbated and extra-masturbated by melting ice-caps we de-cap the vein-popping of the mad male and let cooler heads of blowjob hotties prevail.

So now our Gnostic naughty-talk bans pronouns. Only pet names aloud. Cum when you are called….

1. Throat Boat
2. Twinkie Tot
3. Skankenstein
4. Wizard of Ooze
5. Cream-Filled Clitsicle
6. Her man Cumster
7. Cis Teen Chappie
8. Ass Fault Jungle
9. Kindergarten Coprophage

10. Miss Vaginatown

For the frenetic, mouse-like algorithms of marketeers may sputter, while love may teleport and pour the beloved thru shared pores.

For time transmutes. And less and less clearly do boundaries eyeball bodies enhanced beyond flesh, transcending Floor 13 to a trans-dimensional realm of moments sliced and sub-sliced in **Zeno's** temporal-to-tactile paradox of endless endlessness.

For at the end of days, the endlessness of endlessness is endless.

For language, which destroyed the prison of now, is, in turn, dumbstruck by skin.

For what is skin? Not a boundary, but a portal of 5 million pores.

For the epidermis, the largest organ of them all, wraps two into one.

For tears and kisses smeared Rorschach tests of blood and blackest black mascara.

And for, still more, even in TikTok Disneyfication, and a haunted Oz head, drone lovers will soar & hover, grateful in memories the fallen world would kill for.

ARTICLES:

DAS NEUROCAPITAL

Her Santa Quentin Tarantino Sandinista Nazi hunter does more than castrate revenge. Haunted by gender dysphoria, she may justly de-coronate and decapitate pitiless capos.

And, yes, as their calculations seem to approach infinity, their decimal notations count on you being "just a number." But you're infinite. You contain multitudes. Meta THAT, Mark Fuckerberg!!

Jewish maenads join Judith to seduce Assyrian SS officer Holofernes. He's drunk in his tent. He slumps. He has suck-cummed to the compliant command of her furnace-deep throat. Juicy Judy grips his hair, slices his collar, and…

plop-plop

fizz-fizz

oh what a relief it is!

Yes, the DNA of Genghis Khan persists in 1% of the world's men. But raping and pillaging are simply OG memes. More nowsville parasites monetize reverse-symbiotic dreams.

Watch Walt's rat-a-tat-tat virus pollinate in tête-à-tête scourges of "deep state," as the headlines scream: SCOTUS Rules Fascism Constitutional!

CGI influencers redbull-pill the bits of coin theory that blockchain Planet Scorch! Throning the corporation is its Chair, whose inherently dwindling inheritors call the tune. They suffocate in wealth, while well-endowed foundations, puffed in PR greenwash, suck the air out of the balloon.

We're re-frozen neurons in deep-fried ice cream Infernos.

To the victor go the spoils. But by then everything will be rotten.

In equine dualities that put René Descartes before the horse, corporeal reality plows your body and alienates into rancid spirit. The Invisible Man exponentially multiplies: Trillions of suits, fedoras and glasses, but no heads, with shirt cuffs of air, Claude Rains enacting Samuel Becket in bowler hat cycles over and over, but never really OVER.

Plutocrat Lucifer's failed coup d'é·tat, too, murdered progeny like the American theocracy of child rape and forced birth. He de-captivates his daughter in heaven until she births Death.

"Woman to the waist" with fish-tail legs, you shift shape to breed dog toddlers – John Carpenter's Thing-like. You are denied birth control for a body in endless labor. So tough these days to find Cerberus baby sitters.

Therefore, I, Satan, will adopt your baby!

Sin's daughter sisters her mother, inbreeding Robert Towne's Chinatown. The horror head she slashes could be ours. And the father? He too Gorgos Medusa!

CONCLUSION:

Every Moment Is Easter Morning

I share my stone-stare neck when I bardo to manifest a Walt-Barbelo:

1. who captures the male penis to make child.

2. who devours the organ and returns the head-body of the baby.

3. Whose bio-vengeance lifts her as a lopper of heads.

Barbelo, engendered from language, augmented

from neuron mammoplasty interventions, Edened us orgiastic-style through direct experience of Gaean totality, and chemical suppression of primate dominance. Her machine elves ratchet lubricants and lever hard-ons. Without mushrooms this cloud-brain structure trembles into calcified tumor ego.

And Yahweh is an asshole Demiurge you wouldn't even invite to dinner. He stole our light. Aeons Gorgo and Barbelo flow transcendent transsexuals. They reverse-binary deities nicknamed Panoptis The Luminous -- "All Eyes." A face of peacock feathers making baby deities who grow to re-cycle circular sequences.

But all these derivative divinities who infernalize their heavenly higher-ups are like crummy cash-in psychedelic bands who copy the 13th Floor Elevators. And, wouldn't you know it? Mal-deities capitalize on the confusion. They extract wealth from inner worlds. They sell the rights.

So this is why I Walter:

My higher Barbelo, a plethora of Pleromas, inseminates capital with spirit. Books and music. History regathering strains of soul in rocks and plastic bags.

With Son-of-God motor-mouth powers, she escalators the eschatological directive of the race.

And with Star-Child portal probes, she fruitions the once unredeemable.

Evolution has blown a mind of its own.

Not over time, but now!

Here on Easter Island it's always Equinox.

RESURRECT
Danielle Chelosky

I

The first thing I noticed were his eyes. It wasn't the color that was special, really; they were brown like dirt, but disarming and hypnotic. I wondered what his trick was to be this photogenic, to be able to transcend a screen and look so deeply into a camera as if it is a lover. *you have pretty eyes*, I wrote him, hoping we would match. I knew those words weren't even enough to convey what I really meant. I didn't think his eyes were pretty. I thought they were powerful, piercing. But I couldn't say that.

Our first date was at his place on a Sunday night. It was a time in my life where I didn't care much for being alive, and the only time I felt alive was when my aliveness was potentially in danger. So I was buzzing into his apartment in fishnets and a green velvet dress. He swirled angel hair pasta in a pot and then drenched it in olive oil, a simple dish for us, alongside steak, cooked rare. He talked about his parents and the suffocation of their love as I stabbed the oversaturated meat and watched the redness pour out, like blood circling down a drain. He asked me about myself. I could've told him the truth, said that my parents did the same to me, raising me Catholic and keeping me close, always wanting to know what I'd prepared for confession and deciding on my punishments. Instead I said that my parents were fine people who did the best they could to give me the life I wanted. Then I changed the subject back to him. He grew up on a farm where his first loves were animals. He told me about running his hands through the fluffy curls of sheep, feeling a vague sense of revelation; he recalled being a small boy and looking up at a cow like it was God. The world felt so big then, yet also so small, he said, I wasn't sure which to believe. His eyes were glazed over from being so deep in thought and probably from the wine as well. Why did you come to the city, I asked. He blinked, looking like he just woke up. I wanted to find out, he answered. There was a kind of kinetic energy between us, vibrating and divine, that was so palpable and enormous that if I was standing I would've been knocked down to my knees.

He got a phone call when we were making popcorn, preparing to watch a movie. He apologized and went over to another room. I tiptoed to the door to try to listen in, but all I caught was the urgency in his voice, an echo of worry. I moved away, back to the microwave where miniature explosions penetrated the air. I'm sorry, he said, swinging the door open, I'm having a bit of an emergency here, but I can walk you home. Oh, I said, don't worry about it, it's not far. No, it's no problem, and I want you to be safe, it's late, he said. I knew no matter how much I resisted he would insist, whether it be for my sake or the sake of being a good person. What could this emergency possibly be? I wondered. Why couldn't I help? Is it a lie? Did I say something? I had tried so desperately to appear as normal, but maybe I tried too hard. Maybe he noticed I was off. Or maybe he noticed I was pretending, putting on an act. These thoughts raced through my head as we walked the fifteen minutes to my apartment. He kept apologizing, but what was the point? I lit a cigarette and tuned out his voice. I was outside of my body; I couldn't focus on the moment I was in, because I was worried for the future. But I did wonder what passersby thought of us. Did they think we were a couple? They should've snapped a photograph, I thought, memorialized us, immortalized us. I was so certain he would never talk to me again. When we got to my door, he kissed my cheek, a sacred graze. Yet I panicked immediately afterwards because there was a sense of finality in it. I knew I was probably making it up, but it rattled me to my core.

I stayed up in my bed, staring at his profile on my phone. I felt his eyes staring back at me. His voice repeated in my head, a romantic melody that made my fingers dance over myself, then inside of myself moving to the rhythm of his words, his sentences strung together in enchanting sequences, everything he uttered was a perfect hymn. I thought about the way the word God sounded coming out of his mouth; it made me wonder if I had been wrong for questioning my faith. My passion lifted me out of bed and onto my knees. I looked at myself in my oblong mirror, imagining him sitting on my bed thrusting his cock into my mouth. I was getting tender and wet, I could feel it between my legs; I ached to be filled with something, so I grabbed my hairbrush off of my desk and sat it upright on the floor beneath me and slowly squatted and gasped as it slid inside me. I pretended it was him. I heard his voice saying God, not as a name but as an expression of pleasure, the shape of euphoria. I looked into his digital brown eyes as I came, feeling a vague sense of revelation. But I kept going throughout the night, bending over my desk, my back against my wall, laying sideways on my bed, he fucked me in every possible position and he didn't even know it yet.

He called me the next day in the afternoon. At that point, I figured I would never see him again, that the emergency last night was an intricate plan to evacuate me, that he decided to ghost me. He greeted me with an apology again, atonement gushing from his voice. I received some awful news, he told me. I offered my apology then, and said if he wanted to talk about it that I was there to listen. I applied no pressure. My ex-girlfriend, he said, she's been threatening suicide, and last night was a close call. She's in the hospital now. God, I said, that's awful, I'm glad she's OK, let me know if either of you need anything. Thank you, he said, because of this I'll probably need space for a few days, which is what I called to tell you, but know that it's not you, I really do want to see you again, I mean it.

I could barely sleep that night. I wondered how I ever lived without him. I was reborn that Sunday night. I needed him like I need skin and pores;

without him, I was ugly, a skeleton, an outline of a human. I lifted my feet towards the ceiling, laid my legs against my wall, and penetrated myself with my hairbrush like that, staining my entire room with the stench of sex. Outside cars honked and the wind whistled, harmonizing with my moans and his burdened baritone: I really do want to see you again, I mean it. God. I mean it. God, I mean it, God.

I pictured him showing up at my door. What are you doing here? I'd ask. I couldn't stop thinking about you, and the way your pussy would feel, he'd say, I have a feeling you'd be tight, that you'd feel like Heaven. I wanted to find out.

My dreams were interrupted and delirious. I was half-asleep in my crisis, immersed in a vision where he was about to call me so I had to stay awake and be ready to pick up. I tossed and turned, sometimes licking my fingers and rubbing my clit in an attempt to calm myself down. But I was inconsolable. The next day, I trudged to the cafe to kill time. I sat outside and sipped my coffee while smoking a cigarette. I watched couples pass, giggling and holding hands, inhabiting their own little worlds. No one looked at me, it's as if I was a ghost. I pulled out my phone and started Googling him. I'd been suppressing this compulsion for long enough; this was a way I could hold myself over, quench my thirst. His Instagram, I found out, hadn't been active for the past year or so. I walked through the museum of his past. Pictures of his ex were still there. She looked like me: pale, thin, black hair, existentially fucked. I stared at her, and her eyes were as potent as his, a drug. In broad daylight, I traced her features with my finger as if she were a sculpture I wanted to feel, exhaling smoke, while a couple next to me were discussing their plans to go to Las Vegas over spring break. Her profile was tagged, only a click away. I reached a roadblock immediately; she was on private. However, there was a link in her bio that led to her OnlyFans.

I went home. I sat on my bed and let my finger hover over the link. I wanted to find out.

I made a fake name and bought the cheapest plan. All of a sudden, I unlocked her, I was inside of the most vulnerable parts of her, and she had no clue. After walking through the museum of his past, I was sitting in a pornographic movie theater, getting a glimpse of what he liked. I was getting to know him better. And quickly I started to understand. She was like an animal, the way her moans erupted like howls, the way she moved swiftly and magnificently like a puma, the way her eyes looked up at the camera with innocence and purity like a puppy's. If I were him, I would've done everything I could to satiate her hunger, to fill her up.

But couldn't he see that I was hungry? The hours passed, feeling like years. I walked to the pet store and bought a leash and a collar. As I handed it to the cashier, I had a feeling he could tell that I didn't have a dog. Back at home, I wrapped it around my neck and attached it to my bedpost. I propped my phone up on a pillow and imitated the movements of her hips. I was dripping all over my hairbrush, which I hadn't used on my hair for days; I looked back at myself in my oblong mirror, and knots cascaded down my back, a dark, tangled cascade. The top of my head was like a bird's nest, wildly frizzy. Or maybe it was more akin to a crown of thorns. I was waiting for him to crucify me.

I really do want to see you again, I mean it.

I jolted awake the next morning at sunrise from a nightmare. I was stumbling through a foreign landscape, encircled by a sea of towering trees on a cloudless day. It was summer, but nighttime and humid, so incredibly humid that my mouth was like cotton, I was trying to cry just so I could let the tears fall into my mouth but they wouldn't come out. As I got further on my shadowy path, a sound seduced my ear, colossal and brisk like a river. I started laughing, relieved, exhilarated, approaching the music, and then suddenly, I blinked, I squinted, I saw an army of wolves surrounding me, their steps and collective movement sending the current. They lurched at me, and that's when I gasped for air, sweating, nearly jumping.

My second day without him. I will survive, I told myself. I smoked cigarettes out my window, unable to muster up the courage to leave my apartment. I attached myself to my bedpost again and watched her on my laptop for better quality. She wore a cross on her neck that sometimes stabbed her collar bone. I bet he pressed his lips and tongue against her neck and bit in, wanting more than anything to leave a mark. I bet he trailed down to the space between her breasts and felt holy there, like his mouth belonged eternally at the epicenter between her nipples. I bet he felt like a God there. Or I bet he looked up at her like she was God. I'm sure she did look like God, her eyes two black holes, better than suns, inviting him inside rather than radiating outward. I bet her lips looked like the whole world. I bet the revelation he felt then was not at all vague, but certain and definitive, undeniable, crystal clear.

I wanted to find out.

No wonder this girl tried to kill herself, I thought, she oozed a passion that was uncontainable, she was overflowing with eroticism, she was an animal who couldn't survive amongst humans. I understood her. I understood him through her. I desperately wanted him; I wanted him to show up at my door, smother my mouth with his hand, press me against the window in the living room, strip me, and shove himself inside me without even asking, I wanted people in the building across to see, and people looking up from the sidewalk, and God, and I wanted him to fuck me hard and force me onto the floor and push my face against his cock to swallow his come. I wanted the imprint of my body to be ingrained in the glass in the shape of a sloppy cross.

I needed him like I need skin and pores; without him, I was ugly, a skeleton, an outline of a human. I needed him to hold my hands behind my back and give me no choice. I wanted to be deprived of my personhood, but only by him.

In the afternoon, I walked to the church around the block. I got there as the bells rang, their loud reverberations dancing in the air. I slipped into a pew toward the front. No one looked at me, it's as if I was a ghost. I wondered if my stain showed. Did my fingers still carry the stench of sex, my hair still encircle my head like a crown of thorns? I felt like a fraud there, I felt utterly sick to my stomach, I shuffled out and puked on the sidewalk, a puddle of rot. Was I purged of him? Was I purged of this exorcism of desire? Or was this just the beginning? I sprinted home, humiliated. I was not ready to be a saint, not even ready to try to be redeemed or forgiven. I stood in my kitchen and fucked myself with the handle of a big metal spoon against my refrigerator. Then I finally ran a bath, baptizing myself in the water, cleansing my skin and pores, making my hair limp. I used shampoo and conditioner and ran my hands through the clumps, restoring order. I put the shower head between my legs and moaned. I floated through my filth feeling close to a revelation. I thought of his brown eyes, the resemblance they possessed to my father's. I thought of my father's brown eyes looking into my eyes with such intention, unmistakable certainty. When men are like animals, they are predators with a plan. When women are like animals, they are messy and hysterical prey. We are stuck in this predicament. But there's more agency in pretending as if you've chosen your position, rather than being automatically assigned it. I wanted to know his plan for me, and I wanted to aid in its execution.

But my pretending had gone too far. I lost control; I was possessed no matter what I did. Church failed, my baptism failed, I looked at his profile, I wondered what his trick was to be this photogenic, to be able to transcend a screen and look so deeply into a camera as if it is a lover. Did I ever even meet him? I wondered. Was he just an apparition, a daydream? But I had proof of him in our conversation, which I scrolled through. *you have pretty eyes*. I stared at the phrase and its permanence, like an epitaph.

The first thing I said to him was a lie.

And what if he was celestial, an angel? Maybe he noticed I was pretending, putting on an act. Maybe he had a sixth sense for that kind of thing. I decided I was doomed; my destiny was Hell, a place I wasn't sure if I believed in, but the idea solidified in that moment, an orange, shadowy landscape, burning hot, so incredibly humid that my mouth was like cotton, and I bet my lips would perpetually be chapped, splitting and dripping with flecks of blood, I bet I'd be choking on smoke when a sound would seduce my ear, colossal and brisk like a river, and I'd start laughing, relieved, exhilarated, approaching the music, and then suddenly, I would blink and squint, and I would see an army of wolves surrounding me, their steps and collective movement sending the current. They would lurch at me. What then? Would I not wake up, but be torn to shreds? Would I be penetrated with the slicing pain of teeth? Would I taste the brink of death, but then live, just to have it repeated over and over eternally? Is that punishment?

As a kid, I asked my father what the difference between penance and punishment was. He told me penance was more noble; since it's self-inflicted, it means that you own up to your shame and you want to fix your mistakes and become better. Why does punishment exist then? I asked. He said that some people don't want to become better. Most people, actually.

What if new shame stemmed from your

penance? What if my filth was in my fixing?

After a rough night of sleep, I was skipping breakfast to watch videos of her and perfect my fucking. I found strength in this dedicated fasting. I had to do stretches to make my limbs more flexible. I was being reborn. I contorted my body into inhumane shapes; I could have a savage silhouette, free of the constraints of personhood. I came like a force of nature, a river flowing through the valleys of my thighs.

On the verge of a revelation, so close to Heaven and so close to Hell, my phone rang. I knew it was him, because I erupted like a flood. I ascended on the third day, resurrecting. And then I caught my breath and then I picked up. Hello, I said. Hey, he said, it's me. I laughed, a casual and charming song I'd been practicing. Yeah, I said, it's you.

The world felt so big then, yet also so small.

II

As a kid, I thought my father's brown eyes were the eyes of God. I saw them when I closed my eyes. I saw them when I dreamt, two big suns, radiating a thick brownness, the color falling onto me and drowning me. I saw them watching me always. No matter how desperately I longed to escape their gaze, I was stuck.

He told me over the phone he needed some more time. I heard the crash of a wave that destroyed the world.

I didn't know what I had been thinking. I didn't know why I let relief sink into me like a drug when I saw his name on my phone and then heard his voice in my ear. I should have had my guard up, should have expected the worst.

I'm sorry, he said, she's really not doing well, and I have to do everything I can to make sure she's OK, and I'm not really doing well with all of this either, really. You don't even want to see me right now. I'm a mess. I said, I know what that's like, trust me, don't worry about it. I said, but it sounds like you need someone to take care of you also, so let me know and I'll be there.

Thank you, he said, that's very tempting. I don't doubt that you would make me feel better. I'll let you know.

The comedown began as soon as he hung up, and, as if on cue, my landlord called me to let me know I was behind on rent. I knew. I knew I needed to get a job, and I didn't want a job; I didn't want to be alive, but now I had to be alive because I was waiting for him to let me know and how was I supposed to know when he would or even if he would? Sweet salvation when his name lights up on the screen, like I'd summoned a spirit I'd been meaning to talk to.

Was I not the prey, but the predator? This thought swirled through my mind when I considered the crimes I'd be willing to commit to have him as my own. But I wanted him as my own predator. I didn't want to own him; I wanted him to own me. I wanted him to tease me and hurt me. I wanted to be his target, his emotional outlet.

I took a shower and left the building in search of a new life, a new vessel through which I could survive. I talked to restaurants about food prep or dishwashing, but they only wanted hostesses and waitresses, and that's not what I wanted, I wanted something where I could work passionately in my solitude, away from people.

My past was looking me in the face. I called an old friend about the possibility of me returning to my old job, where he still worked. He asked me where I'd been. I took this as an acceptance back in.

And so I spent days in a dim Bed-Stuy apartment hunched over a stove with a clunky mask encumbering my face and making me look like a human-sized fly. My hands moved carefully, covered with tight, thick gloves, mixing together colorless substances that emitted stenches so pungent that there were piles and piles of towels by the bottom of the door. It was me and only one other person, and we rarely spoke; we stayed safely undistracted, only disrupting the silence with low volume jazz, which in itself was a kind of silence. Our movements were meticulous, they had to be, or else they would be lethal.

At home, I began eating again, only because I needed the energy food gave me in order to work. I could no longer languish away as I had desired to. I swirled angel hair pasta in a pot and then drenched it in olive oil, a simple dish, alongside steak, cooked rare. I stabbed the oversaturated meat and watched the redness pour out, like blood circling down a drain. I thought about the way he sliced the tender, dead thing and talked about the animals on farms as if they were holy. Is that what you do to holy things? I should have asked him. You put them over a fire to heat them up, and then you cut them with a knife and swallow them? I shook my head, lost in these spiraling contemplations as if I were really back in that moment, reliving it. Instead this time I was not drawn to him. I resented him. It was only temporary, a flare-up of hostility. Then I retreated back into my adoration like I was returning home.

These were the only places where I felt safe. Inside of a love that was at the epicenter of passionate rage and deep devotion; inside of a job that could go up in flames at any moment, or send me to jail for a sentence close to life. The possibility of danger soothed me.

By the time my creation was complete, it had all been worth it. A batch like little shards of glass, like icicles kicked onto the ground by a little kid, like healing crystals in a bowl at a spirituality shop. I understood, then, the urge to ingest it, to want to be infused with its secret powers. I would also trust a material so beautiful. I did this over and over and over; sometimes it became so tedious and the saxophone sounded like it was mocking me with its luscious, sprawling vibrations, but at least it kept my mind off him. There were days where I didn't even want to leave the apartment and I wished to sleep on the couch knowing that there were unknown stashes beneath me. I grew comfortable in the armor wrapped around my head; I treasured this anonymity, I was no longer me, no longer woman. I was a soldier in nuclear war. I didn't care about things like love or lust. I was sexless. I was surviving.

I'd begun seeing a psychoanalyst. I felt all of these repressed feelings crawling under my skin and I wanted to tear them out of me. He was a lot older than me, this man whose voice hummed like a heater, trying to give me warmth so I would feel comfortable enough to unleash the unspeakable. I sank into the velvet green loveseat across from him, always starting with a stiff posture, and then easing into releasing the tension in my body.

My first session was tormenting. How does someone begin something like this? There's no easy way. It wasn't until the third session that I brought up the painful longing I'd been experiencing. What's his name? He asked. Let's call him Aaron, I said. I could not reveal his actual name because I did not like the way the syllables felt in my mouth, the way it reduced him to a mere sequence of letters. What do you like about him? He asked. What a ridiculous question. I could not think anything except: What a ridiculous question. I muttered some qualities that attracted me to him. I liked his eyes, his voice, his kindness.

The session after that, he handed me whiskey in a glass. He asked again: What do you like about him? He knew I had been lying. I said: I don't know, there is something about him that won't leave me alone, I am so deep in that I don't think I will be able to get out.

Do you normally have these periods of obsession? He asked. Do you think there's ecstasy in the idea of your obsession never being satiated? Are you fixating in order to ignore trauma? Is there something from your past you have to face?

Our safe word was window. I said it when I felt incapable of answering a question, or if I needed a break. I said it, window, window, window, it began to lose meaning, and my alcohol-stained tongue slurred slightly, widow, wow, dew, wind, why, wow.

At my job, the one other person I worked alongside spoke to me for the first time. We're not gonna be here much longer, he said. It was around the middle of the day. It sounded as if he wasn't even saying it to me, but just acknowledging the inevitable to himself. He knew more than

I did about that gig. He knew who we worked for, where the drugs went, how the money was distributed. I trusted that he was right, but I wasn't sure what my next move was.

I was contemplating this, my next move, when he called. I didn't know how long it had been. Every day was in slow motion in that dim Bed-Stuy apartment, and my psychoanalysis appointments only blurred time more. I was walking home when the staccato buzzing against my leg startled me. It was a sensual pulsating, throbbing. I knew it was him.

The sky was pitch black and the streets were vibrant with clamor and color. This all registered as my phone rang, as if waking me up. I realized it must've been the weekend, or close to it. The air was no longer sticky; there was a slight breeze, leading me to believe summer was coming to a close. Hello, I said.

Hi, he said, one syllable, so contained like he was afraid. I've been thinking about you.

Have you? I asked curiously, neutralizing my tone to try to maintain an innocence, a small sense of surprise.

I expected some update on his ex-girlfriend, his ex-girlfriend whose flexible body sometimes popped up in my mind at work threatening to distract me with her allure, and I'd have to push her out immediately, a reflex that helped me on my stride forward.

But he did not even mention her. He invited me to his place, a return, where maybe our night would be uninterrupted, maybe we would stay together as the clamor and color of the streets relented, maybe we would get to know each other's bodies while the city around us slept, maybe we would watch the sun rise, maybe we could exist as one as the world ran its course.

I walked in circles before returning home, thinking about my frustration with our love. I put so much time and effort into it, and where did that all go? It didn't turn into a crystal, like it did at my job; it was invisible, painfully intangible. How could we know it was even there? I had delusional fits over something that could not even be seen or touched.

Before work the next day, I trudged to the cafe again. I sat outside and sipped my coffee while smoking a cigarette. I knew time, today and tomorrow, would stand as still as car crash traffic. All of the moments in front of me were like brake lights. It was so torturous; I felt like I was handcuffed while someone dangled pleasure over me. I arched my body upward to try to reach it, but I couldn't, the object of satisfaction was out of my control. I was paralyzed in my desire.

The one other person I worked with was not there. I dawdled around for a moment, wondering if I should've done something about that. But there was nothing I could do. My hands moved carefully, but I was dancing to the sound of silence, rather than the low volume jazz. It was a dangerous quietness, daunting. I wanted to be excited about seeing him again, but I couldn't shake this sense of finality. I thought a beginning was supposed to come.

I went to my psychoanalyst that night with the intention of lying. I would not tell him about our plans. I knew he wanted me to overcome my obsession and acknowledge all that I was hiding within myself. I had wanted that, too, before he was back in my life. Now I wanted to return to the safety of my desire.

He fixed me whiskey again. He leaned toward me, and I saw his face close up, the grey hairs in his beard, the creases in his forehead, the splits in his lips. His eyes were an electrifying blue, like crystals or bolts of lightning. I noticed the look on his face was not as detached and serious as usual; he looked curious, even amused, as if I were some kind of zoo animal. When I finished my whiskey, he refilled it without my asking.

Aaron is not the name of this man, he said, but it is the name of a man in your life, correct? He asked, like some kind of psychic.

I stiffened, submitting to a wave of tension. I sipped my whiskey. Window, I said.

We've had enough sessions, he said, to the point where we're not using a safe word anymore. Safe words are to help a patient ease into the process. You are not supposed to feel safe here. You sacrifice your safety to feel better in the long-term.

We're not gonna be here much longer, I thought to myself. In that moment, I made an internal promise to never see him again. I would focus on the only places where I felt safe. Inside of a love that was at the epicenter of passionate rage and deep devotion; inside of a job that could go up in flames at any moment, or send me to jail for a sentence close to life. What was I doing in this office, looking outside of myself for answers that are within myself? Maybe I just liked the idea of giving the power over to someone else, of letting someone dominate my subconscious.

Aaron is your father, correct? He said, his certainty palpable, as it usually is with men.

Window. He refilled my whiskey. Is obsessing over this man a kind of penance for the shame of what happened with your father? Do you feel shame for what your father did to you? Are you having trouble distinguishing shame from penance? Window. Did you think you were going to come here today and not answer any questions? Do you think I can't force your answers out of you? Window. Window. Window.

I took out a little bag from my back pocket and spilled the contents out onto the table. I crushed the crystals into dust, a tragic change of form, and I snorted it. Go ahead, I said, shivering and gasping, alone on a numb, jittery plane, elated and grey. The room, illuminated with a soft orange glow, faded and spun, and I could feel my hands lift above my head. I could feel the metal enclosing around them, keeping them tight together. And then I felt pins and needles on the lower half of my body, which seemed so far away from me as if it was an attachment of myself rather than a part of me. I was being filled up, and there was a big hand on my neck, knuckles penetrating my chin. I coughed with pleasure, as if I was being purged, purged of this exorcism of desire, purged of myself.

I woke as the sun came up. I was fully clothed, sprawled out on the loveseat, alone. I got out as soon as possible. I trudged to the cafe and I sat outside and sipped my coffee while smoking a cigarette.

I've been thinking about you. I really do want to see you again, I mean it. God. I mean it. God, I mean it, God. God.

Everything was far away then. Him, God, the psychoanalyst, my father, the disappeared colleague, besides, what were the differences between any of them? I wondered, then, about the ex-girlfriend. How was she, her holy hips? Was she getting better, or was she just plotting to kill herself again? Once you commit to death, I thought, you have to keep trying for it. The more it eludes you, the more alluring it becomes.

He felt so far away, yet I was seeing him that night. I wondered how long I would have to shower to cleanse the stench of sex off of me. I still was coming down from the drugs and the alcohol, and it was as if life was pouring out of me, like blood circling down a drain. I was fading.

On autopilot, I moved methodically, suppressing all thoughts of last night, pushing away flashbacks, but it was completely silent without the jazz, and his voice repeated in my head. You are not supposed to feel safe here. Safety, I realized, was not real anyway. Safety was an illusion we projected onto people and places for our own sake. Safety was the ultimate selfishness. I basked in the intensity of our love because the core of it was safe, spacious and stretchy like a trampoline, but the edges were sharp, threatening to cut me. The first time someone threatened to cut me I was a kid, and I let him because I was supposed to put my trust in him and let him take care of me, and my blood was evidence of our bond, tangible, something that could be seen and touched. That was love.

I kicked the stove and I tore the mask off of my face. My cheeks were wet. I was alone in this fit, but I felt the presence of everyone beside me, of disappeared colleague, of my psychoanalyst, of God, my father of him, my object of desire who I was supposed to be seeing that night, but I could sense that that wasn't going to happen because everything felt so far away, I was above myself, like I was becoming God, and becoming my disappeared colleague, becoming my psychoanalyst, becoming him, everything and everyone merged. All of a sudden, the unbearable, disorienting silence was broken and I was brought back to earth. A sound seduced my ear, colossal and brisk like a river. I started laughing, relieved, exhilarated, approaching the music, and then suddenly, I heard a booming noise, an enormous banging on the door, and yells whose words I could not make out. I looked around me, covered in sweat and tears. I wasn't sure what my next move was, and I had no time to figure it out. I was paralyzed by everything and everyone in that moment. The door was torn down then, ripped from its hinges, and a congregation of men in uniforms surrounded me like an army of wolves, their steps and collective movement sending the current, vibrating the floor. Before they could lurch at me, I lurched first, and I was high as I flew, soaring out the window. I closed my eyes, summoning up a picture to admire as I fell to my death. The last thing I saw were his eyes.

TALENTED PERVERTS ™

Talented Perverts is a wholly owned subsidiary of Filthy Loot Enterprises.

Shane Jesse Christmass - Meth-dtf
Charlene Elsby - Letters to Jenny Just After She Died
Ira Rat - The Medication
Alex Osman - Scandals
Various - Little Birds (green)

**PERPETUAL
NOSTALGIA
FOREVER** ®

www.ingramcontent.com/pod-product-compliance
Lightning Source LLC
LaVergne TN
LVHW092057060526
838201LV00047B/1441